AF394354

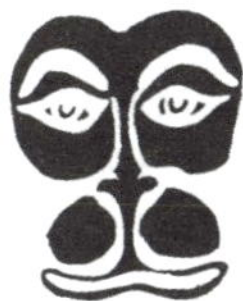

INSISTENCE AS A FINE ART

Enrique Vila-Matas

TRANSLATED BY KIT SCHLUTER

HANUMAN EDITIONS

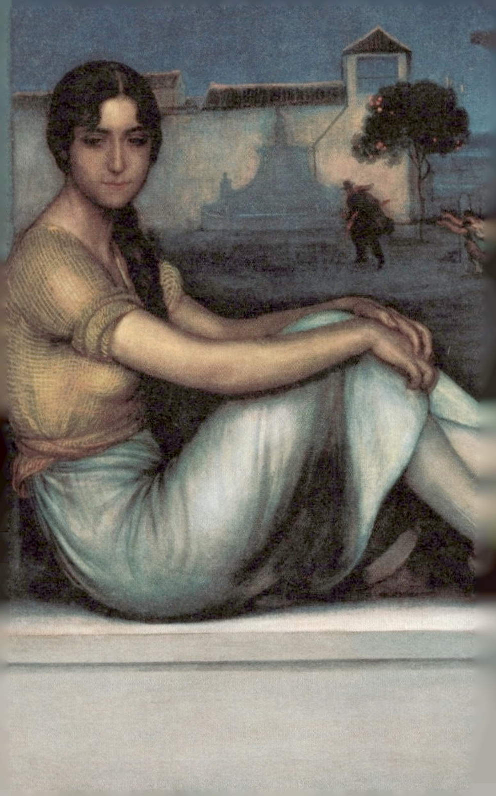

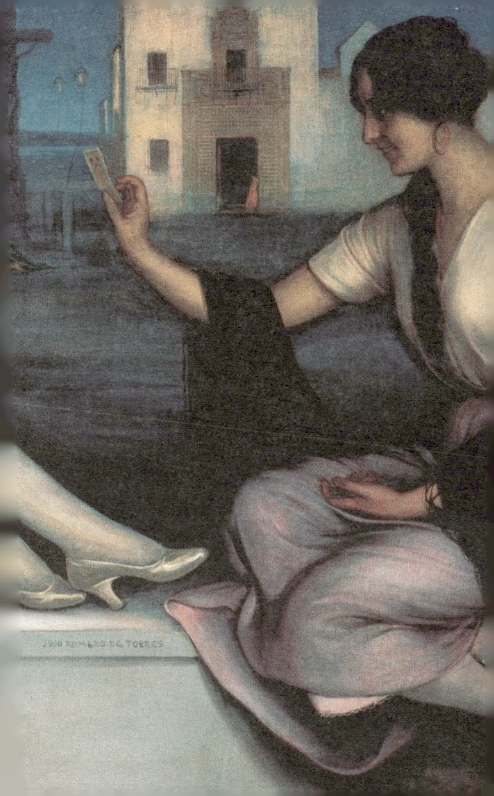
JULIO ROMERO DE TORRES

Insistence
as a Fine Art

1.

This morning, via WhatsApp, I received an article by Ramón del Valle-Inclán in which he protested Julio Romero de Torres's exclusion from the prizes of the 1912 National Exhibition of Fine Arts.

"The selected artists were buttered up, prizes auctioned off, a jury thrown together and rigged with the selfsame brazenness with which a minister of Governance rigs the meek herd of a parliamentary majority in the so-called Temple of Laws. Among the artists participating in this exhibition, the only one who appeared to be master of an aesthetic was Julio Romero de Torres. A subtle aesthetic that seeks in his subjects that mysterious gesture capable of transforming them into unique and enduring things."

It seemed to me that the secret of the classics lay hidden in this last sentence. Not much later, another article arrived via WhatsApp. Like the first, its source was Ana Rodríguez Fischer's monumental archive. In it, Antonio Machado spoke of Romero de Torres in highly laudatory terms on the occasion of his passing. His comments struck me as related to Valle-Inclán's words on

the awful treatment the painter
received among certain Spanish
circles. Indeed, when he learned
of Romero de Torres's death,
Machado put down in writing
that he had been a great painter,
a man of extraordinary kindness,
and the humblest artist he had
ever met. "He died forgotten by
all of these new people. His
painting, nevertheless, will
endure."

The new people then, I thought,
were probably like some of the

new people now: they despised everything they didn't know. And just then, the phone rang. They were calling from Málaga, urging me to choose the painting from the Thyssen Museum's permanent collection that I would like to speak about in the talk I had agreed to give there on January 23.

I had almost made up my mind, but I still had some doubts. I was wavering between Joaquín Sorolla and Julio Romero de

Torres. The former was that great artist devoted to light. And the latter seemed to me a better fit for establishing common ground with my writing, although I might end up needing some of Sorolla's light to finally convince myself that I already knew what to choose. In the end, the Málagans' urgency brought things to a head, and the praise from the truly great Valle-Inclán and Machado tipped the scales in favor of the Cordovan painter. In fact, I had already practically foreseen that, one day, when the phone rang and they urged me to name the painting I'd chosen, I would pretend to be unsure— I enjoy that kind of inside joke— and, shortly after, reinforcing my decision with simulated doubt, name, almost automatically, as if the answer were being given by a machine connected to the forces of the universe, Romero de Torres's *La Buenaventura* (*The Fortune Teller*).

That mysterious gesture that

renders artworks unique and enduring, the gesture alluded to by Valle-Inclán, was surely key to my choice of that painting from 1920 (there's another from 1922, by the way, which is very similar and shares the same title).

Working with all the freedom in the world, I decided to exemplify "that mysterious gesture" with one very concrete detail of *La Buenaventura*: the woman holding up a playing card frozen in the course of time.

There are two young, dark women in the painting, each bearing her own enigma, bringing life to an eternally enlivened frame. And this afternoon I felt so strongly that I had caught a glimpse of eternity in that motionless gesture that I suddenly even felt that eternity itself, with its infinite and congenital quietude beyond time, had just been set down before me. "For I love you, O Eternity!" I recalled that Nietzsche had once written.

2.

Nietzsche's phrase, when it appeared among my thoughts, left me momentarily stunned. What could the philosopher have meant? And why, as I looked at a work by Romero de Torres, did the German thinker steal across my mind?

To better understand this, I reflected on Nietzsche's intuition that man is a being whose nature consists, precisely, in continuous self-overcoming. The idea seems to be at odds, I thought, with the admiration we feel for those who love to remain faithful to themselves, the artists who, out of fidelity to their own poetics, insist on exploring what interests them so keenly, and for that reason insist and insist and return to it and create the misunderstanding that they have no

interest in overcoming themselves, when it's really the other
way around, since the ones who
insist on grasping what they
know will resist their efforts
offer us the clearest evidence
of a continuous will to self-
overcoming.

The case of John Banville, for
example, is paradigmatic. Once,
during a talk, he had to answer
a question from a woman in the
back row, who asked him sharp-
ly when he planned to stop

writing about men who kill women. He replied with Irish composure: "When I get it right, I'll stop doing it."

I come back to Nietzsche's "For I love you, O Eternity!" to be sure that it really was irrelevant for me to have snuck it into a commentary on a Cordovan painter the German never could have heard of. In the same way, the epigraph with which Alberto Savinio opens his book *Maupassant and the Other* makes no sense.

The epigraph was from Nietzsche and read, "Maupassant, a true Roman."

Savinio, ever astute, added in a famous footnote, "I'm not at all joking when I say that Nietzsche's definition really does shed light on the figure of Maupassant, albeit by way of absurdity. The phrase becomes even more illuminating in so far as what Nietzsche meant by calling Maupassant 'a Roman' remains ambiguous. Perhaps he didn't mean anything at all, as often happens in his work. But will the reader understand me if I say that the more you say, the more you say nothing?"

Anyhow, I communicated the title of the chosen painting, *The Fortune Teller*, to Málaga and I thought for a while about that scene of eternity contained in Julio Romero's work. A scene of eternity, though paradoxically framed by the painting's restricted form. And I began to suspect that I would never know exactly what it was he was narrating to us in that painting, beyond what it seemed to be narrating. But I think that's normal. Because, despite its appearance, this is a work of art so complex, so close to the absolute, that, as happens with certain of Nietzsche's phrases, it allows for all interpretations and, at the same time, none.

The card dealer's gesture is singular because it can be isolated from the rest of the painting and remain equally mysterious. In the end, it seems to contain the enigma of the Andalusian soul. The woman showing the five of coins is someone of positive and optimistic character and, what's more, someone who knows what is going to happen. This last point is even more enigmatic and connects with prophetic artworks such as, for example, the Saint Vincent Panels on display at the National Museum of Ancient Art in Lisbon. These six panels, attributed to Nuno

Gonçalvez, contain the enigma of the Portuguese soul. They are disquieting, because they prophesy the Age of Discovery and show us that they were painted by someone who *knew what was going to happen*, which is to say, the era of great splendor which lay in store for Portugal.

I've spent the whole day struck by that moment when, on the phone, I named *The Fortune Teller* almost automatically, as if the answer were being given by a machine connected to the forces of the universe.

The more I went back to look at the chosen Romero de Torres painting after I'd named it, the more I felt convinced that it would fit in well beside works that, deliberately or not, refuse to remain always the same and prefer to rise up against any interpretation, being aware, most of the time, that disassociation from the world's complexity is a misstep—a point proven, I should note, by the overwhelming length of the sentence I will now conclude.

Tomorrow will be a new day, a new day for this personal diary.

3.

It goes without saying that I'm
an activist for Multiplicity.

Yesterday, after naming the cho
sen painting, I returned to the
friendly combat which, from time
to time takes place within me:
an argument between Lightness

and Multiplicity, two of Italo Calvino's six well-known proposals for the literature of this millennium. For a long time, all my youthful "portable theories" were framed by Lightness, whereas lately the theories drawn from my activism have been fitting in with the other extreme, Multiplicity.

It's a friendly confrontation, since Calvino's two most attractive proposals coexist perfectly inside me. In the sector of Lightness is the lightly-packed suitcase of youth, that stage during which, being "portable", one feels comfortable in groups, whereas in Multiplicity, as it coincides with one's final years, one achieves a feeling of being "as if inside oneself at last" (as Gil de Biedma said, speaking of Cernuda).

As if inside myself at last. That could be the name of the kind of solitary activism that, after the interruption of the phone call, I engaged in only yesterday, and which, as I tried to find the lost thread and remember what it was that I was thinking when they called from Málaga, I ended up remembering that I was wondering how *The Fortune Teller* would be if it were literature.

Did I find an answer? No, but the answer was that Romero's painting could easily be included in the idea of Multiplicity, alongside the work of Carlo Emilio Gadda, that master of representing the world as a great net. Or rather, that master of representing the world as a tangled mess, a ball of yarn, an immense knot, a monumental clutter, or as an Odradek, that confusing, flat, star-shaped spool covered with pieces of thread which Kafka discovered for us.

Not for nothing, Gadda was the pope of Multiplicity. And the question arises: could that confusing spool be Multiplicity itself, or its opposite, a simple ball of thread, something like a forgotten world? Were the latter true, we would have to accept that this Odradek or a lost world would be a useless and inoffensive object, covered in loose threads, forgotten on some old staircase of an unknown pantheon. Gadda was implacable with the world and represented it in his books without attenuating its inextricable complexity or, for that matter, diminishing the simultaneous presence of the most heterogeneous elements that coincide in any and all manifestations.

In my particular case, and per what I've been writing here in this diary, I would say that some of the heterogeneous elements that influenced me when I chose *The Fortune Teller* were: the kindness and genius of the underappreciated Cordovan painter; Nietzsche's absence; a playing card frozen in the course of time; my activism on behalf of the Multiple; the landline phone;

loose threads hanging from a homemade Odradek; the world as an infinite knot; and a fleeting glimpse of eternity on Earth.

4.

It turns out that thinking of Gadda yesterday was useful, since he fits perfectly into my complex plan to try to convey the multiplicity of interpretations offered by *The Fortune Teller*, a more involved painting than it may appear at first glance.

Gadda would have lost himself in it, or with it, he would have found infinite motives for writing a novel with no possible ending, as happened in the case of Musil, the German Gadda, and Lezama Lima, the Cuban Gadda. Then Perec and Bolaño came along with novels that had no endings either, but all this now belongs to the history of Multiplicity that somebody, someday, will write.

Even Julio Romero de Torres

himself would get lost if he were made to see—if he weren't already aware of them—the multiple, inexhaustible interpretations offered by *The Fortune Teller*. I like to picture him looking at his work with the same gaze that underlies his "subtle aesthetic", modestly telling anyone who sought an absolute meaning in his work that he had always been aware that, whenever he commented on his own paintings, he was merely explaining the most facile part, whereas the more interesting thing really was everything that evaded explanation, given that it was precisely that which made the work a point of obsession for certain of its observers. It has always been impossible to be a good artist and at the same time to feel capable of explaining one's own work intelligently.

5.

This afternoon, while I still had a headache from last night's trip through the invisible—an unexpected modality of nightmare, which I hope doesn't make a habit of visiting me—they called again from Málaga, this time to see if I might give them advance notice of my talk's title. I didn't expect the request to arrive so soon, just a few days after having chosen *The Fortune Teller* as my subject.

I put myself in Orson Welles's shoes when, in a Boston train station, his producer, Harry Cohn, asked him over the phone to let him know the title of the movie he was planning to shoot.

Welles, who hadn't yet planned a thing, let alone a title, was saved when he noticed the cover of a lowbrow novel displayed on a newsstand beside the telephone booth. The title was *If I Die Before I Wake*, signed by one Sherwood King. There was a brief silence, which Welles broke by instructing Cohn to buy the rights immediately. And so it was that from a very mediocre novel came *The Lady from Shanghai*, widely considered a classic film.

Suddenly, seeing myself as Orson

Welles in Boston, I broke my silence and, with the rhythm of a machine gun manufactured for multiplicitous acts, said:

"Insistence as a Fine Art."

I was well aware of what I was saying, but as soon as I pronounced it I feared I might become prisoner of the title once the time came to do it justice. Shortly after, however, I thought that I, as an activist for Multiplicity, would have ample enough space in which to move around and so shouldn't have any problems. Besides, I thought to myself, supposing I should find that the title had to change as I went along writing, it would always be possible to do so. It would probably suffice to simply appeal to the audience's understanding, and everything could be changed without issue.

When, from the other side of the line, they applauded me for being so quick, I didn't mention

that Luísa Casa, a Cordovan
from Barcelona, had explained
to me two days before that if
there were one inescapable
concept in Romero de Torres's
work, it was repetition. And this,
Luísa said, was well documented
in Fuensanta García De La
Torre's analysis of *The Fortune
Teller*, which she sent me by
e-mail.

6.

Repetition? Therein lies, I thought straight away, the nexus of connection I had been seeking between Romero de Torres's painting and my own writing, in which repetition has always played an important role. Repetition viewed in a positive light.

Kierkegaard was able to see its supremely attractive side when he said that repetition and memory were the same movement, only in opposite directions, "since what is remembered is repeated moving backwards, whereas repetition, strictly speaking, is remembered moving forward. That's why repetition, if such a thing does exist, makes man happy, while memory leaves him bereft."

I had read *The Fortune Teller's*

first repetition in Fuensanta
García De La Torre; it was in
the title itself, since there was,
in fact, another painting known
as *The Fortune Teller*, kept in a
private collection, painted around
1922, two years after the one that
concerns us here today. The subject of this second *Fortune Teller*
was the same as the one from
1920—two women sitting on
a windowsill with a view of
Córdoba with its Fuente de la
Fuenseca, the Marquis de la
Fuensanta del Valle's palace, and

the Christ of the Lanterns behind them—but in this other *Fortune Teller*, the woman receiving the reading of her marvelous future fortune was lying down nude. As for the composition, the clearest comparison could be found in the portrait of Conchita Torres (Madrid, private collection), painted around 1919-1920. The painter inverted Conchita's poisition, also sitting on a windowsill, transforming her into a young woman for whom a painful heartbreak lay in waiting and working in a few differences, limited to her outfit and gaze. The other female figure was missing, but the landscape and architectural background were the same, only without the Christ of the Lanterns, and the background scene, the secondary scene, had been altered. The deck of cards would also be repeated as a motif in other works, although imbued with a very different meaning than in the first *Fortune Teller: The*

Fortune Teller of 1922, *The Sibyl from the Alpujarra* (Córdoba, Romero de Torres Museum, 1911); *Smoke and Chance* (painted in 1923 to decorate the tobacco and lottery shop on Madrid's Calle de Alcalá); *The Card* (Madrid, private collection); *Old Woman's Head* (Córdoba, Romero de Torres Museum, 1928), and he may have intended to include it in the unfinished *Women on a Shawl*, as well.

I remember how, while I was transferring Fuensanta García De La Torre's information, it began to seem to me that the framing of all those paintings depicted two women who may indeed have been a single one in which two distinct manifestations of her character coexisted; one woman, a beautiful Andalusian who mixed melancholy with the optimism of every possible fortune telling, receding, on the one hand, with nostalgic sorrow, and, on the other, moving

forth with the joy of repetition
which always accompanies such
forward movement.

7.

This afternoon I started thinking again about how the painters of Insistence and Repetition generally use a limited number of figurative elements, in fresh combinations, although placing them in different roles in each work. This is true in the case of

Romero de Torres, who works with a deliberately restricted deck of cards with which he nevertheless plays many games, equally creative and boundless in their approach. His different versions of *The Fortune Teller* dance around that magic deck. I think it would be fair to speak of a "Fortune Teller series". Each of these paintings narrates a story quite similar to the others, but unique, as well, with its own enigmatic general idea; considered together, they attain an overall unity.

Their overall unity runs parallel with that of my literary work, since the latter is really just one single book, composed of the various books I have written and which together form, as Felicidad Juste would have it, a single volume: "a poetics understood as the exercise of a literary discourse which, together with the theoretical ideas it generates, creates, in fact, a complex conceptual structure." A structure which experience has told me can cause among its blunter readers the impression that I am merely repeating myself without using repetition as a way to move forward. And it's really quite the opposite: I repeat myself in order to move forward. It wasn't for nothing that I decided to join the Brotherhood of the Insistent. To project myself into the future, forever with the motto, "When I get it right, I'll stop doing it."

8.

"We are born, and insistence already exists", I recalled having written once at the beginning of a sort of timid manifesto in which I exposed my vision of murder and repetition as two of the fine arts.

We are born, and insistence already exists. And this is something to which, for example, cinema has attested ever since the moment of its invention: the Lumière brothers were unconvinced by their first version of *Workers Leaving the Lumière Factory* and, cognizant of the fact that continuous repetition would be unavoidable in this new art, they shot the same sequence twice more, refining it each time.

There's no shortage of antiquated

minds who denounce insistence on a theme. They did so back in the day with Romero de Torres. And one senses that they'll soon be criticizing people for lingering on a paragraph in a book or drawing the same mountain many times.

And even so, insistence lives on.

Not long ago, I noticed this in the stunning fifteen-or-so minute opening scene of Béla Tarr's film *The Man from London*, based on the Simenon novel. The Hungarian director made me feel that I myself was suddenly up in the port-side watchtower where he had placed the eyes of the camera and his protagonist: a lookout, an observer, insistent like no other, a recorder of everything his sight could capture from the top of his tower. And what it captured was various, so various that he even witnessed a crime. A murder. A blow, a man falling dead into the water. The camera remained still, with

Hungarian insistence: the sequence's morose rhythm did not modulate once the falling form splashed into the water. And everything continued in the night, in the night where everything was going on as before. Not even the background changed: a grey character with a panoramic view of the watchtower, fog, smoke, "Simenon moments", the tension of a port. And in the background, the incalculable force of a passion for insisting on what one seeks.

9.

When I woke up, I imagined a
hypothetical *History of Obstinate
Acts*, in which the following
things played an important part:
the many occasions on which
Romero de Torres placed a
playing card in a new context,
the Christ of the Lanterns,

twilight, the most famous fountain in Córdova, two feminine figures that occasionally give the impression of being two primary masks of the same woman, one single person.

Also prominent in the speculative History were the numerous times when, over the centuries, humanity insisted on asking the question of how many things could be painted. In modernity, the question has been flipped on its head: is there anything that can't be painted? I suspect that Romero de Torres, a prime candidate for Multiplicity, was capable of painting everything and capable, moreover, of covering up this tendency by enacting a poetics that reduced the number of figurations, remaining with no more than the two indispensable dark women, two masks, perhaps two angles on a single woman, who is attempting to feel finally alone, unique, "as if inside herself at last."

10.

At the fair of Insistence and Repetition, the lord and master is
Cézanne, who carried obstinancy
and insistence to remote land-
scapes of the mind. He painted
the Mont Saint-Victoire eighty
times. Among stubborn painters,
he was the stubbornest.

I remember that there were already many people at the end of the last century who found a great mystery in the question of how Cezanne's repetitive practice came into being. Wim Wenders, for example, offered an answer, as if thinking aloud: "With a pencil and watercolors and on paper, of course, but that doesn't answer the question of what Cezanne's gaze was like."

And "what Julio Romero's gaze was like" while painting *The*

Fortune Teller is precisely what I've been thinking of the past several days leading up to this one, on which I've come before you to read the fragments from my diary that discuss the background of my talk.

What was Romero de Torres's gaze like when he painted the different versions of *The Fortune Teller*? It would not be strange to find that it was kindred to Cezanne's, with his eighty mountains: an emotional and analytical gaze all at once. The painter sees (and shows us) something that moves him deeply; at the same time, he dissects it.

But how can these two elements be combined? Looking at *The Fortune Teller*, where both elements—emotional and analytical intelligence—also merge, I think I can answer that question: it was painted with a spirit to dissect the world and at the same time charge it with emotion and life. It demonstrates such care, desire, precision, tenderness, and fascination that it's something that only a lover can embrace, someone who loves with his entire soul the multiplicity and radical beauty of a scene that describes and analyzes, with light, the true magnitude of the South.

11.

NOW BEFORE THE PUBLIC

As if inside myself at last, now before the public and in the fiction of the moment, a nod to Valle-Inclán: "Romero de Torres's paintings offer us, in the fiction of the moment, a glimpse of the gesture in which all things are frozen as if in a state of ecstasy." It's not lost on me that, if you trade in the comfort of writing in your office for the risk of a public appearance, you have to come away convinced that the best thing you can do is read what you have written at your desk and know that you will continue to write in a way that is always as free as possible. The singer Janis Joplin was well aware of this last point. Once, on that very staid TV of the 60s,

the deeply American host asked
her if it was true that she had
once said that her audiences
experienced a sort of weird trip
when listening to her music.

The studio audience cracked up
when they heard the question,
probably because the phrase
"weird trip" made it sound like
he was speaking in Martian.

"Well, yeah," Janis answered.
"There's probably a barrier
between the audience and me,

but when I see them dance I
realize they're dancing with me.
You give and they receive, even if
it's hard for them sometimes.
From that moment on, you can
sing more and more freely."

That's what it's all about: using
entirely new maneuvers to feel,
somehow, that one is writing in
an ever freer way, and that this
kind of novelty, however crazy
it may seem, leads me to see in
The Fortune Teller, if I insist, per-
spectivesthat I may not have

been able to anticipate when I
first approached the painting.
In fact, shortly before I came
into this courtyard, when I
saw—with the insistence of an
activist for Multiplicity—the
Fuente de la Fuenseca standing
in the background of Romero de
Torres's painting, it seemed to
me that it stood at the very
center of the dramatic scene the
author had created: the fountain
as unstoppable energy, as source
of the series of endless changes
that were taking place during

that moment in the history of painting. Because in 1920, when Julio Romero made *The Fortune Teller*, Cubism, considered the definitive rupture with traditional painting, had already faded, but was giving way to the rest of the European avant-gardes of the past century.

The Fortune Teller is neither a classical nor a modern painting, but a mixture of both, as if its secret motivation had been to combine the avant-garde and the classical. Alongside our difficult, complete deciphering of the scene which Julio Romero depicted (opening himself up to the world's complexity and infinitude), we perceive in the background the painter's commitment to a method of understanding, a fresh search for a potentially totalized network of connections between the facts, people, and things of the world. Julio Romero's proposal was dominated by a certain critical anxiety that fortified associations between tradition and contemporary "rupture", a proposal always in the difficult shadow of the search for old ideas that appear new.

Romero de Torres painted half-way between the past and the future, halfway between classical art and the modern art that was to come, two arts that may have seemed irreconcilable except if, as Julio Romero did it, they were created lucidly in a fleeting pre-sent in which the two possible

lives of painting were already
beginning to intermingle.

The Cordovan master painted
with the rhythm of the present,
of the lived moment, with our
rhythm of right now. The case,
Borges said, is that all things
happen to us precisely, precisely
now: "Centuries upon centuries,
and only in the present do things
happen; numberless men in the
air, on land and on sea, and all
that truly happens only happens
to me."

ABOUT THE AUTHOR

Barcelonan writer Enrique Vila-Matas is among the most prominent contemporary Spanish authors, a renown that makes him no less avant-garde. He studied law and journalism, worked as an editor on the film journal *Fotogramas*, and lived in Paris between 1974 and 1976.

Vila-Matas is the author of the prize-winning *Dublinesque* (2010), which along with his numerous short stories, essays, columns and articles, conveys a deeply intertextual commitment to the construction of writing. Vila-Matas' work has been translated into 32 languages and awarded numerous prizes, including the 2001 Premio Rómulo Gallegos and the prestigious Prix Médicis for the best foreign novel in France, in 2003. The author belongs to the Orden del

Finnegans, whose members are committed to veneration of Joyce's masterpiece *Ulysses*.

ABOUT THE TRANSLATOR

Kit Schluter is author of *Cartoons*, a collection of stories and drawings, and *Pierrot's Fingernails*, a book of poems. Among his recent and forthcoming translations are booka by Rafael Bernal, Copi, bruno darío, and Marcel Schwob. He has long lived in Mexico City.

Insistence as a Fine Art
Enrique Vila-Matas

Published by
Hanuman Editions
London & Seattle
hanumaneditions.com

Founding Editor: Shruti Belliappa
Co-Editor: Joshua Rothes
Editorial Assistant: Moselle Kleiner

Publishers: Shruti Belliappa, Joshua Rothes
Design: Shruti Belliappa, Joshua Rothes
Typesetting: Joshua Rothes

Opening illustration, *La Buenaventura*, Julio Romero de Torres, 1922

First Edition. First printing.

ISBN 979-8-9904165-0-5

Printed in the UK on Fedrigoni Arena Natural.

Typeset in Arnhem Fine, with Eksell and Caslon No540 Swash D.

Hanuman Editions is designed, edited, and published by Shruti Belliappa and Joshua Rothes, in friendship.